GREETINGS FROM SOMEWHERE

The Mystery at the Coral Reef

BY HARPER PARIS • ILLUSTRATED BY MARCOS CALO

LITTLE SIMON

New York London Toronto Sydney New Delhi

LITTLE SIMON

An imprint of Simon & Schuster Children's Publishing Division · 1230 Avenue of the Americas, New York, New York 10020 · First Little Simon paperback edition July 2015 · Copyright © 2015 by Simon & Schuster, Inc. All rights reserved, including the right of reproduction in whole or in part in any form. LITTLE SIMON is a registered trademark of Simon & Schuster, Inc., and associated colophon is a trademark of Simon & Schuster, Inc. For information about special discounts for bulk purchases, please contact Simon & Schuster Special Sales at 1-866-506-1949 or business@simonandschuster.com. The Simon & Schuster Speakers Bureau can bring authors to your live event. For more information or to book an event contact the Simon & Schuster Speakers Bureau at 1-866-248-3049 or visit our website at www.simonspeakers.com. Designed by John Daly. The text of this book was set in ITC Stone Informal. Manufactured in the United States of America 0620 MTN 10 9 8 7 6
Library of Congress Cataloging-in-Publication Data
Paris, Harper. The mystery at the coral reef / by Harper Paris ; illustrated by Marcos Calo. — First edition. pages cm. — (Greetings from somewhere ; #8) Summary: With help from their cousin Harry, eight-year-old twins Ella and Ethan discover who is illegally taking coral from the reefs near their aunt and uncle's beach house on the shore of Australia's Coral Sea.
[1. Brothers and sisters—Fiction. 2. Twins—Fiction. 3. Coral reefs and islands—Fiction. 4. Family life—Australia—Fiction. 5. Australia—Fiction. 6. Coral Sea—Fiction. 7. Mystery and detective stories.] I. Calo, Marcos, illustrator. II. Title. PZ7.P21748Mww 2015 [E]—dc23 2014026235
ISBN 978-1-4814-2371-7 (hc)
ISBN 978-1-4814-2370-0 (pbk)
ISBN 978-1-4814-2372-4 (eBook)

TABLE OF CONTENTS

CHAPTER 1
Australia!

"That girl's going to fall off the bridge!" Ella Briar shouted.

Her twin brother, Ethan, looked up. The Sydney Harbor Bridge gleamed against the bright blue sky.

At the top of the massive bridge was a girl peering over the side. How did she get all the way up there?

And then Ethan saw that there were

other people with her. *Lots* of other people.

"It's okay, kids. You can actually climb to the top of the bridge," their father, Andrew, explained.

"The view is supposed to be great!" their mother, Josephine, added.

"Wow!" Ella gazed out at the sky-line of downtown Sydney and at the sailboats that dotted the harbor.

The view from the top of the bridge probably *was* great. But she couldn't imagine being up that high. She'd had enough of high places after Machu Picchu!

Machu Picchu was an ancient Incan city in Peru that was thousands of feet in the air. The Briars had spent

some time there before flying off to Australia. Australia was the seventh stop on their trip around the world. Mrs. Briar was a travel writer. She was writing about their adventures for their hometown newspaper, the *Brookeston Times*.

The twins were excited to be in Australia. It was beautiful and warm, plus everyone spoke

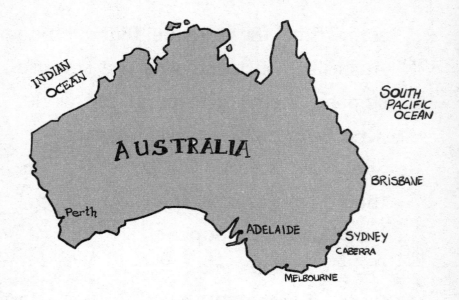

English, which meant that it was easy to communicate. Best of all, they were driving up the coast tomorrow to visit their aunt Julia, their uncle Owen, and their cousin Harry.

"Who's hungry for some Balmain

bugs?" Mr. Briar called out.

"*Bugs?*" Ethan and Ella gasped in horror.

Mr. Briar laughed. "They're not actually bugs. They're a kind of lobster. I thought we could check out a seafood restaurant for lunch."

"And after lunch, we'll go *there*." Mrs. Briar pointed to a white building that jutted out into the bay.

Ethan squinted. The building looked like a row of stegosaurus spikes. "What is it?"

"It's the Sydney Opera House. We'll do a backstage tour and then stay for the opera," replied Mrs. Briar.

"What about the aquarium?" asked Ella. "Hannah's family went there last summer. She said it was awesome!" Hannah was Ella's best friend back in Brookeston.

"I wish we could fit that in. But we won't have time today. And we're leaving Sydney first thing tomorrow morning," said Mrs. Briar.

Ella pouted. Ethan was disappointed, too. He had really wanted to experience some real live sea creatures while they were in Australia! Hopefully there would be another chance for that.

CHAPTER 2

The Redthroat Emperor

"Are we there yet?" Ethan groaned.

"This is bo-ring!" Ella complained.

It was Thursday, and the Briars were driving up the coast to a city called Brisbane. For the first couple of hours, the twins had enjoyed staring out at the passing scenery: the sandy beaches, the turquoise sea, and the pretty fishing villages. But after nine

hours, they were more than ready to get out of their cramped little rental car.

"We're almost there," Mrs. Briar assured them from behind the wheel.

Mr. Briar spread a crinkly map across his lap. "I think we turn off at the next . . . Oops, wrong map! This is a map of Italy." He dug through his backpack and pulled out another map. "Okay, here we go. We stay on this road until you reach a town called Surfers Paradise. And then we turn inland."

"That means away from the

coast," Ella explained to Ethan.

"I know what 'inland' means," Ethan snapped. "That was one of Dad's vocabulary words from last week." Mr. Briar was homeschooling the twins while they traveled.

It was almost dinnertime when the Briars finally arrived at their destination. Their aunt's family, the MacLeans, lived just outside of Brisbane. Their house was built on stilts and had a red tile roof. The front yard was filled with palm trees and lush grass.

17

Aunt Julia rushed out the front door. "Hello. Hello!" she called, waving excitedly.

"Jules!" Mrs. Briar hugged Aunt Julia for what seemed like forever. The two sisters hadn't seen each other since the MacLean family moved to Australia five years ago.

Aunt Julia turned to hug the twins. "The last time we saw you, you were only a few years old. Ethan, I hear you're a soccer player. And, Ella, you're writing poetry?"

Ethan and Ella smiled and nodded.

Inside the house, Uncle Owen and their cousin Harry greeted everyone.

"Welcome to Australia, mates!" Harry said with a wide grin. At fifteen, he was almost as tall as his father. He wore a T-shirt that had a picture of a surfer on it and lime-green board shorts.

"I hope everyone is hungry!" said Uncle Owen cheerfully.

Ella noticed that both Uncle Owen and Harry had Australian accents, but Aunt Julia didn't have an accent at all. It was kind of funny!

The four grown-ups went into the

kitchen to prepare dinner. "Do you have a computer?" Ethan asked Harry. "Ella and I need to check our e-mail."

"Sure! You can borrow Billabong Bill," replied Harry.

"Uh, Billabong Bill?" Ella repeated, confused.

"That's what I named my laptop," Harry said with a wink.

A few minutes later, the twins
sat on a couch in the family room
with Billabong Bill between them.
Harry sat on the floor, polishing a
surfboard.

After a moment, an e-mail popped

up from Grandpa Harry! He was Josephine and Julia's father. The twins' cousin Harry had been named after him. Ethan and Ella were used to seeing a lot of their grandfather back home, and they really missed him.

Hello, my dears. Welcome to Australia!

I received your most recent e-mail, about your time in Machu Picchu. I was happy to learn that you found the Temple of the Sun as well as the special artifact that your grandma Lucy and I came across long ago.

And now you are in the "land down under"! Did you know that you are very near the largest coral reef system in the world? Coral is amazing because it's a living organism! It can look like a rock or a plant, but it's actually a kind of animal.

Coral reefs are an important habitat for fish and other species. It's against the law to remove coral from reefs in that area. However, there have been many reports of people doing just that.

When your grandmother and I visited Australia, we went snorkeling in the Coral Sea. We saw sea turtles, whales, and of course, lots of fish! As a souvenir, I bought her a necklace with a sea turtle pendant on it. She gave it to your aunt Julia to keep.

Please give my love to everyone! I wish I could be there with you all.

Love,

Grandpa Harry

PS If you get a chance to visit the coral reefs, keep an eye out for the redthroat emperor!

Ethan and Ella stared at each other. Keep an eye out for the redthroat emperor? What in the world was the redthroat emperor?

29

CHAPTER 3
A Ticking Watch

The next morning Aunt Julia and Uncle Owen had a big surprise for the Briars.

"Guess what? We're going to spend the weekend at our beach house!" Aunt Julia announced.

"It's on the Coral Sea," Uncle Owen added.

"The Coral Sea?" Ella tried to

remember Grandpa Harry's e-mail from yesterday. "Is that the one with the coral reefs?"

Aunt Julia smiled. "Yep, that's the one!"

"Hooray!" the twins shouted. They would finally get to swim in the ocean. They couldn't wait!

A few hours later, the two families arrived at the MacLeans' beach house. It was a wooden cottage surrounded by palm trees. Just beyond the backyard was their private beach, which meant that no one else could swim there.

"Look!" Ethan said, pointing. A sleek gray creature jumped out of the water and arched in the air. It was a dolphin!

Uncle Owen suggested that they all take a walk on the beach.

"Not me. I'm going surfing with Rufus and Tommy," Harry announced. He scooped up his surfboard and took off down a dirt path.

"Be careful!" Aunt Julia called after him. "We worry about our Harry. He's a bit

of a daredevil," she told the Briars.

"What's a daredevil?" asked Ethan.

"A person who likes to do *daring* things," replied Mr. Briar.

Ethan nudged Ella. She nudged him back. They liked to do daring things, too—like going on adventures and solving mysteries. The three cousins must have gotten that from Grandpa Harry!

All the parents started down the beach. Ethan and Ella trailed behind. They kept their eyes on the sand, searching for seashells and other treasures. Ella was eager to find a shark's tooth to add to her collection back home.

Waves curled up to the shore and slipped away, leaving small pools of water filled with pebbles and seaweed. Ella spotted something shiny in one of the pools. Could it be a shark's tooth?

She bent down to pick it up. It wasn't a shark's tooth. It was a watch!

She turned the watch over in her palm. It was heavy. Inscribed

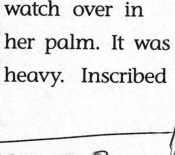

on the back were the letters *ZD*.

"*ZD*. Those must be the owner's initials," Ella said out loud. She thought for a moment. "Hmm. That means the watch doesn't belong to Aunt Julia, Uncle Owen, or Harry."

"Yeah, but who could have dropped it here?" Ethan asked when he overheard Ella. "This is a private beach, right?"

Then Ella noticed something else. "Ethan, the watch is still ticking!"

"Whoa!" Ethan exclaimed. He paused. "Wait, what does that mean?"

"It means that the watch probably hasn't been in the water for very long," replied Ella. "Whoever dropped it could have been here yesterday or even today!"

CHAPTER 4

Three Mysteries?

Around noon, Aunt Julia drove Mrs. Briar, Ethan, and Ella into town for some shopping and sightseeing while Uncle Owen, Mr. Briar, and Harry stayed behind to do some fishing. The town overlooked the Coral Sea. There were restaurants, stores, and an open-air market with stands that sold everything from local crafts to fancy jewelry.

Ella had brought the watch along in her bag. She wasn't sure who it belonged to or why it had washed up on the MacLeans' private beach. But she was determined to find out. She and Ethan were good at solving mysteries. In fact, they had solved

mysteries in each of the countries
they had visited so far: Italy, France,
China, Kenya, India, and Peru.

The two sisters stopped at a stand
to admire a display of necklaces.

"Look at this one. Isn't it lovely?"
Mrs. Briar held up a strand of

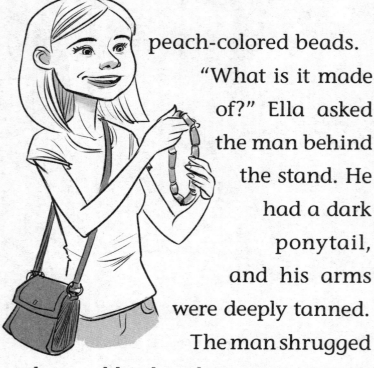

peach-colored beads. "What is it made of?" Ella asked the man behind the stand. He had a dark ponytail, and his arms were deeply tanned. The man shrugged and waved his hand at a sign. It said: CORAL COLLECTORS.

Aunt Julia scanned the table, which also displayed bowls, mirrors, and animal figurines. "You have a lot of items for sale, and they're all made of coral. Where did your coral come from?" she asked.

"We, uh, have our sources," the man mumbled. "Now, if you'll excuse me, I'm very busy." He turned his back and began digging through a crate.

"He's not very friendly," Mrs. Briar said to Aunt Julia as they moved on.

"I've never seen him here before. He must be new," Aunt Julia replied.

"I really do wonder where he got all his coral. It's illegal to mine coral from the reefs around here, you know."

The four of them continued walking through the open-air market. While the others were looking at T-shirts, Ella sat down on a bench. She reached into her bag and pulled out her purple journal and a pen. The journal had been a present from Grandpa Harry, and she used it to keep notes. A lot had happened in

the last twenty-four hours, and she
wanted to get it all down on paper.

She opened the journal to a fresh page and began writing:

> We found a watch on Aunt Julia and Uncle Owen's beach.
> It has the initials "ZD" on it.

She thought for a moment, then added:

> Grandpa Harry said: If we visit a coral reef, we should look for a redthroat emperor.

She also added:

We just met a man selling coral jewelry and other stuff. Where did he get all that coral?

Ella paused to read over what she had written. She blinked in surprise. Did she and Ethan have *three* mysteries on their hands?

CHAPTER 5

An Intruder!

That night Mr. Briar, Mrs. Briar, Uncle Owen, and Aunt Julia decided to go out to dinner in town while Harry stayed at the beach house with Ethan and Ella.

"I left you guys a cheese pizza and some cut-up veggies on the kitchen counter," Uncle Owen told the twins. "We should be back around ten. There's a cricket match on the telly, if you're interested."

"A cricket match?" Ethan pictured a bunch of crickets hopping around.

"You're in for a treat, kids! Cricket is a terrific game," Mr. Briar said eagerly. "It's similar to baseball, and it was first played in England four hundred years ago!"

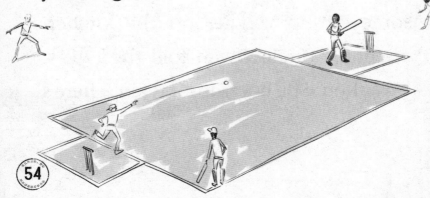

After more instructions, the parents took off. The twins went into the living room to find Harry. The "telly" was on, and the cricket match was under way. But Harry was nowhere to be seen.

Ella peered into the bedrooms. "Harry?"

"He's not in here, either," Ethan called out from the kitchen doorway.

They searched all around the house, but there was no sign of Harry. Where did he go?

"But I just saw him, like, ten minutes ago," Ella said, confused.

"Maybe he went out with his friends and didn't tell anybody," Ethan guessed.

"We should probably call Mom and Dad

on their cell phone," Ella said nervously. It was dark outside, and they were all alone in a place they didn't know.

Just then, the door from the garage burst open. A figure stalked in,

wearing a strange mask.

The twins screamed.

"Whoa! It's me, mates!" The person took off the mask. It was Harry!

"You *scared* us!" Ella cried out.

"Not me. I wasn't scared," Ethan said quickly.

"Sorry! Didn't mean to frighten you.

This is my snorkeling mask," Harry explained.

"Why are you wearing a snorkeling mask?" asked Ella.

Harry smiled, a twinkle in his eye. "Because we're all going for a night swim!"

CHAPTER 6

Snorkeling After Dark

"Awesome!" Ethan exclaimed. After all, he and Ella *had* wanted to see real live sea creatures.

"Is it safe?" Ella asked.

Harry chuckled. "I've gone snorkeling at night a million times! Besides, you two seem like adventurous types."

Ethan beamed. "We are *super*-adventurous."

"But what about our parents?" Ella pointed out.

"No worries. We'll be back before they get home," Harry replied.

Ella glanced over at her brother. Ethan shrugged. A night swim *did* sound like fun.

A short while later, the three of them stood on the beach dressed in slick black wet suits. Harry had found a couple of his old ones for the twins. Palm fronds rustled in the cool breeze. A cloud passed over the moon.

Harry had also given the twins some snorkeling equipment: a mask,

a snorkel, and a water-proof headlamp. The mask was clear and covered the eyes and nose. The snorkel was a mouth tube that would allow them to breathe when they dipped their faces in the water. The headlamps were attached to bands that wrapped around their heads.

Ella shivered as she gazed out at the end-less black sea. It was

so *dark* out here. Even with the head-lamps, she couldn't imagine seeing anything underwater except for more darkness.

"Okay, mates. Turn on your headlamps and follow me," Harry instructed.

The twins clicked on their head-
lamps. Harry waded into the shallow
water, and they followed. It was cold
at first, but after a minute, they got
used to the temperature.

Harry showed them how to put
their faces in the water as they swam.
He also showed them how to breathe
through their snorkels.

They all began swimming
with their faces down. Their
lamps made shimmery paths of
light in the murky water.

They could see fish . . . dozens of
fish! There were yellow ones and red
ones and blue ones and rainbow ones,
too. It was incredible!

Harry pointed to a school of

jellyfish. They glowed pearly white as they swam gracefully toward a row of orange rocks.

Except that the orange rocks weren't rocks at all. They were coral! Fish drifted in and out of the coral, feeding on algae and plankton. Sea stars clung to the sides. Crabs and lobsters crawled along.

"Wow!" Ella started to say. But with the snorkel in her mouth, plus being underwater, her word just came out as tiny bubbles.

Ethan gazed in wonder as a sea turtle swam out from behind the coral. Then he noticed something near the turtle. A thick rope dangled in the water. A heavy-looking anchor

was tied to the end of it.

Ethan tilted his head up. At the top
of the rope, he could just make out the
bottom of a small boat.

Ethan frowned. A boat? At this time of night?

Ella had noticed the boat too. So had Harry. He motioned for the twins to follow him back to shore.

Back on the beach, they observed the boat from a distance.

"I thought this was a private beach. What's that boat doing here?" Ethan whispered.

"Not sure," Harry whispered back.

Ella thought she could just see a couple of words painted on the side of the boat. Both words started with a C. The other letters were hard to make out, though.

Splash! A man suddenly swam out of the water and climbed onto the boat. Another man followed, and then another.

All three men were dressed in scuba gear. And they carried bulky nets.

"What's in those nets?" Ella whispered.

Harry squinted. "It's hard to see. It looks bumpy and orange. I wonder if it's—"

"*Coral!*" the twins said at the same time.

CHAPTER 7

The Coral Thieves

The boat's engine revved loudly as one of the men started the motor. Suddenly, the boat swung in the direction of the beach. Ella, Ethan, and Harry ducked behind a large rock so they wouldn't be spotted.

As the boat turned to speed away, Ethan peered out from behind the rock. He glimpsed one of the words on the side of the boat. It was: COLLECTORS.

Once the boat was gone, the kids hurried into the house. They changed into dry clothes and threw their wet things into the dryer. After all, their parents could come home at any minute. Then they met back in the living room.

"I can't believe those guys were

taking coral from the reef. We're supposed to protect the reef, not steal from
it," Harry said, shaking his head.

Ella reached for her bag and pulled out her journal. She opened it and wrote:

> Three men stole a bunch of coral from the sea. Their boat had two words on it. Both words started with the letter "C."

"What is that, homework?" Harry asked curiously.

"No. It's, um . . ." Ella snuck a glance at Ethan.

"Ella likes to take notes whenever we're solving a mystery," Ethan blurted out.

"*Ethan!*" Ella cried out. Their mystery-solving work was a secret.

Harry grinned. "Gnarly! Can I help?"

Ella thought for a moment. Maybe it would be okay to confide in Harry. He was their cousin, after all.

"Well, some weird things have been happening," Ella began.

"You mean, before tonight?" Harry looked surprised.

Ella nodded. "Yesterday we found a watch on your beach. It has the initials *ZD* on it."

"Hmm. There's no one around here with those initials," Harry said after a moment.

"Then this morning we met a guy in town," Ethan went on. "He had a stand with coral jewelry and stuff. He wasn't very friendly."

"And now we have the three coral thieves," Ella finished. "Their boat was named C something, C something."

"I got a good look. One of those words was 'collectors,'" Ethan added.

Ella leaned

over her journal and wrote:

C_____COLLECTORS
COLLECTORS C_____)

Ella glanced up, her eyes shining. "The coral stand. It was called Coral Collectors!" she exclaimed.

CHAPTER 8

A Secret Plan

"Maybe the guy at the coral stand was one of the guys we saw on the boat just now," Ella went on.

"Yeah, and he had his accomplices with him!" Ethan added.

"His accom-what?" Harry asked.

"An accomplice is someone who helps you commit a crime," Ethan explained.

"I just thought of something. Maybe the watch we found belongs to one of those three guys. Maybe they were here stealing coral and the watch fell in the water," Ella suggested.

Ethan's face lit up. "And *I* just thought of a plan to catch them!"

* * *

The next morning, Ella and Ethan asked their parents if they could go into town again.

"But we were just there yesterday," Mrs. Briar said as she sipped her coffee. "Besides, your aunt and uncle thought they would take us snorkeling."

"Your mum and dad said you've never snorkeled before. You're going to love it!" Uncle Owen piped up.

"Um . . . ," Ella stammered. The four grown-ups had no idea that she and Ethan had gone snorkeling last night with Harry. She had to come up with a good reason to go into town instead. "Could we snorkel later? I, um, saw a pretty bracelet at one of the stands. I want to buy it for Hannah's birthday. I have money from my allowance!"

After some discussion, the families came up with a new plan. Uncle Owen and Mr. Briar would drive the three kids into town while the moms went for a morning swim. Uncle Owen said that he needed to buy some new fishing gear, anyway. Then they would all go snorkeling in the afternoon.

The twins, Harry, Uncle Owen, and Mr. Briar arrived in town just after ten o'clock. The sun was already high in the sky, and the open-air market was crowded with tourists in shorts and bathing suits.

Harry offered to take the twins around the market while the dads went to the gear shop. "We'll meet you there in fifteen minutes," he said.

"Sounds good!" Uncle Owen put his hand on Mr. Briar's shoulder as they turned to go. "Maybe we can pick up a couple of breakfast pizzas on the way. I know a great little stand."

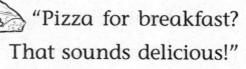

"Pizza for breakfast? That sounds delicious!" Mr. Briar said excitedly.

Harry and the twins headed over to the Coral Collectors stand. It was all part of the plan Ethan had come up with. Ella pulled the watch out of her bag and handed it to Harry. "It'll fit you better than Ethan or me," she whispered.

"Got it." Harry slipped it onto his right wrist.

At the coral stand, the man with the ponytail was arranging coral figurines on the table. He was the same man from yesterday. A gray-haired woman in a Hawaiian-print dress stood nearby, snapping pictures.

Ella walked up to the table and picked up a coral bird. "Isn't it cute?" she said to Harry.

Harry took the bird from her and pretended to study it. Ethan noticed

Mr. Ponytail staring at Harry's watch.

"W-where did you get that?" the man asked Harry.

Harry flexed his wrist. "This watch? Pretty sweet, isn't it?"

Then Ethan noticed something else. The man had a peculiar tan line on his left wrist. There was a white patch of skin there where a watch would have been.

Obviously, he had stopped wearing his watch very recently. Or *maybe* he'd lost it in the water. . . .

Ethan thought about the initials on the back of the watch: *ZD*.

"Excuse me, Mr. . . . Zach?" Ethan guessed.

"It's Zeke. Zeke Donner," the man corrected him.

Ethan grinned at Ella and Harry. *ZD!*

CHAPTER 9
Long–Lost Treasure

Ethan pointed to the tan line on Zeke Donner's left arm. "Did you lose your watch, Mr. Donner?"

"Why do you want to know?" Mr. Donner asked suspiciously.

"Because we found it on our aunt and uncle's beach!" Ella burst out.

Harry took off the watch and dangled it in the air. "It must have fallen into the water when you and your mates were stealing coral."

Mr. Donner went pale. "Give me back my watch!"

Just then, the gray-haired woman in the Hawaiian-print dress stepped forward and flashed a gold badge.

"Freeze! You're under arrest!"

Ella gasped. The woman was an undercover police officer!

The police officer handcuffed Mr. Donner and then turned to the twins and Harry. "We've been after this man for months. We couldn't find

evidence that he and his accomplices were stealing coral from the sea. Fortunately, I just recorded this entire conversation. We never would have

stopped these coral thieves without your help. Thank you!"

"You're welcome!" Ella said happily.

Ethan started to say something, too—then stopped.

The police officer's badge had a picture of a hawk on it.

Ethan pulled his gold coin out of his pocket. Grandpa Harry had given it to him as a going-away present.

On one side of the coin was an image of a globe.

On the other side was an image of a hawk.

It was weird, but hawks kept popping up during the trip—first in Italy, and now, all the way in Australia.

Was it just a coincidence?

* * *

Back at the beach house, it turned out that Mrs. Briar and Aunt Julia had solved a mystery, too.

"Guess what Jules and I found while we were swimming?" Mrs. Briar announced.

Aunt Julia held up a silver turtle charm that dangled from a delicate chain. "It's Mom's necklace that Dad bought for her during their Australia trip. She gave it to me ages ago. I thought I'd lost it!"

"We noticed it sticking out of the sand," Mrs. Briar explained.

"It was badly tarnished, so we cleaned it up with silver polish. Now it looks good as new!" Aunt Julia gushed.

"It's amazing what can wash up on the beach," Mrs. Briar added. The twins giggled. So did Harry. They were thinking about the watch, which was now in the hands of the police.

"What's so funny, kids?" Mr. Briar

asked as he munched on the remains
of his breakfast pizza.

"You had to be there," replied Ella.

"Yeah, Dad. You had to be there,"
Ethan echoed.

Then Ella remembered something

that had been bugging her. "I have a question. Does Australia have an emperor, like China used to?"

Uncle Owen shook his head. "The prime minister is our leader. We also have a queen."

"Then who is the redthroat emperor?" Ella asked.

It was Uncle Owen and Aunt Julia's turn to laugh. "Not who. *What*," Aunt Julia replied.

"Redthroat emperors are a kind of fish that live in the Coral Sea. They were Dad's favorite when he and Mom went snorkeling here."

"*Oh!*" said Ella.

"Speaking of snorkeling . . . who wants to go?" Uncle Owen called out.

Harry and the twins exchanged a
secret smile. "We do!" they shouted.

CHECK OUT
THE NEXT

GREETINGS FROM
SOMEWHERE

ADVENTURE!

ALASKA, USA

We're going to crash into the mountain!" Ethan Briar cried out.

"That's not a mountain, silly. That's a cloud," his twin sister, Ella, said with a laugh.

Their pilot, Zane, steered their small plane through a thick cloud. For a moment the whole world was white.

Then they reached the other side,

and the snow-covered face of Mount McKinley rose into the sky. Even from a distance, it looked massive!

"Now, that's a mountain," their father, Andrew, said. "Isn't that incredible, kids? It's the tallest one in North America!"

Their mother, Josephine, held her camera up to the window and clicked. "This is quite the view. My readers are going to love these photos!"

Mrs. Briar worked as a travel writer for their hometown newspaper, the *Brookeston Times.* The Briars were traveling around the world so she could write articles about different places.

Alaska was the eighth place they had visited so far. It was very different from their last stop, which was Australia. In Australia, the twins had gone snorkeling in the warm waters of the Coral Sea. Here in Alaska, it was winter, and there was snow everywhere.

Zane circled Mount McKinley several times before nosing the plane down to a nearby lake. He coasted just above the frozen surface. "There's a moose on the shore!" he said, pointing.

The twins craned their necks. An enormous moose gnawed on the bark of a tree.

After Mount McKinley, they headed south. They flew over volcanoes, icefalls, and glaciers. This was the twins' first flightseeing experience, which was sightseeing from the air. It was pretty amazing!

They soon reached Prince William Sound. A dozen seals sunned themselves on a large sheet of floating ice. Ella gazed out the window. "I can't believe we're in the same country as Brookeston," she said in awe.

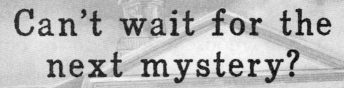

Can't wait for the next mystery?

Find activities, series info, and more.